Who Has Eaten My Popcorn?

by Susan McCloskey
illustrated by Monique Passicot

Harcourt

Orlando   Boston   Dallas   Chicago   San Diego

Visit The Learning Site!

www.harcourtschool.com

Once upon a time there was a little
girl who lived in the woods. Her name
was Goldilocks. Goldilocks loved to
walk. One day she walked very far—
farther than she had ever walked
before. She walked all the way to the
city! "Oh, my!" she said. "This is the
farthest from home I have ever been! "

2

The city was so big! It was the biggest city Goldilocks had ever seen. She stared up at a tall building. Goldilocks had never seen a taller building. "That must be the tallest building in the world!" she said softly to herself.

Goldilocks stopped at a corner where
some musicians were playing loud
music. She put her hands over her
ears. She had never heard louder
music. "That must be the loudest music
in the world!" she said softly to herself.

Goldilocks got tired of the tall buildings and the noise. She walked down a side street filled with small houses. Goldilocks stopped at one house that was smaller than the others. "I like this house!" she said. "It's the smallest house on the street!"

Goldilocks looked in the window. The television set was on. In front of it were three chairs. Next to the chairs was a table with three bowls of popcorn. The chairs looked soft and the popcorn smelled good. All of a sudden Goldilocks felt tired and hungry.

Nobody answered the doorbell. So
Goldilocks walked in. First, she sat in
the big chair. It was nice and soft. Then,
she sat in the middle-sized chair. It was
even softer. Last, she sat in the small
chair. "This is the softest one!"
Goldilocks said. So she sat back to
watch the cartoons.

Goldilocks was very hungry. She
tasted the popcorn in the big bowl. It
tasted good. She tasted the popcorn in
the middle-sized bowl. It tasted even
better. She tasted the popcorn in the
small bowl. "This tastes best of all!"
Goldilocks said. So she ate every bit.

Goldilocks sat back and watched cartoons. The first cartoon was funny. The second cartoon was even funnier. The third cartoon was the funniest of all. Goldilocks laughed and laughed. She laughed so hard that she broke the chair into little pieces!

"That's too bad!" said Goldilocks, as she yawned and stretched. She was so tired! She decided to take a nap. Then she would hurry home. She needed to get home before it got dark outside.

In the bedroom were three beds.
Goldilocks tried them all. The big bed
was comfortable. The middle-sized bed
was even more comfortable. The small
bed was the most comfortable of all.
Soon Goldilocks was sound asleep and
snoring.

Just then the Bear family came home. Papa Bear noticed that someone had been sitting in his chair. Mama Bear noticed that someone had been sitting in her chair, too. Baby Bear noticed that someone had been sitting in his chair. It was broken into little pieces!

Then Papa Bear noticed that
someone had been eating his popcorn.
Mama Bear noticed that someone had
been eating her popcorn, too. Baby
Bear noticed that someone had been
eating his popcorn. It was all gone!

"Who has been eating my popcorn?"
he cried.

Then Papa Bear saw that someone
had been in his bed. Mama Bear saw
that someone had been in her bed, too.
Baby Bear saw that someone was
STILL in his bed. She was making scary
noises! He started to cry and Goldilocks
woke up.

Goldilocks said she was sorry for
making Baby Bear cry. Then she told
the bears that she was very sad to
leave, but she had to be home soon.
She did not want her parents to worry
about her!

The Bear family drove Goldilocks home in their van. She hugged them and thanked them. Papa Bear said, "You're welcome! You must be careful, you know! After all, there might be bears in the woods after dark!" Then they drove home to their little house in the city.